Copyright © 2018 Clavis Publishing Inc., New York

Originally published as *Sammie in de herfst* in Belgium and Holland by Clavis Uitgeverij, Hasselt — Amsterdam, 2017
English translation from the Dutch by Clavis Publishing Inc., New York

Visit us on the Web at www.clavisbooks.com.

Sammy in the Fall written and illustrated by Anita Bijsterbosch

ISBN 978-1-60537-404-8

This book was printed in June 2018 at Wai Man Book Binding (China) Ltd. Flat A, 9/F., Phase 1, Kwun Tong Industrial Centre, 472-484 Kwun Tong Road, Kwun Tong, Kowloon, H.K.

First Edition
10 9 8 7 6 5 4 3 2 1

SAMMY
in the Fall

Anita Bijsterbosch

Clavis
NEW YORK

Sammy made a big pile of leaves.
The hedgehogs like the leaves.
They will use them to build
a warm nest for wintertime.
But where did Sammy go?

It's fall. Sammy and his friend
Hob are picking apples.
Sammy sees a bird.
"Hi, little bird. This apple
is for you," Sammy says.

The trees are beginning
to lose their leaves.
Sammy is raking the leaves.
Hob is playing in the wheelbarrow.

"Peekaboo! Here I am!"
Sammy calls.
Can you find the baby hedgehogs
asleep in their nest?

Sammy likes to take walks in the fall.
He collects acorns and chestnuts
and puts them in his basket.
Hob is coming along for a ride.

Suddenly the wind starts blowing.
"Whoa! It's raining leaves!"
Sammy shouts.
Sammy and Hob run back home.

Sammy and Hob are inside,
where it's warm and cozy.
Time to make some crafts!
Look at the spider web Sammy
is making out of yarn and sticks.

Sammy jumps in the puddles.
"It's raining, it's raining
—but we are not getting wet!"
Sammy sings.

Sammy sails a boat in a puddle.
"Bye, boat. Go sail to
the rainbow," Sammy says.

It has been a perfect fall day.
Before he goes to bed, Sammy
looks at his favorite picture book.
"Look, Hob—what a nice squirrel,"
Sammy says. But Hob can't hear him
anymore. He's asleep already.

Good night, Sammy and Hob.
Tomorrow is another
fun-filled fall day!